USA TODAY BES

A.K. KOONCE

SOUL
KISSED

SOUL
KISSED

To Sophie!

[signature]

Table of Contents

Chapter One

The Realm of Monsters

Rhys

The heat of a blazing beast scorches my flesh. The smell of burnt hair singes my senses, but it all doesn't register as my feet rush faster and faster until the one thing inside me snaps. It cracks away at the panic covering my mind until a wolf snarls up my throat and consumes my body as its own. She turns and faces my fears head-on.

Just as she always does.

But the two-headed monster that looks down on me isn't

something she was ready for. Jagged teeth like glass snatch me up, and the bat flies up fast with me in tow. Smoke covers my vision as I jerk from side to side, going higher and higher with no ground in sight.

My own name is an echo of a roar in the distance as I'm carried away. Torben's rage rattles through me with the sound of his panicked agony calling out among the chaotic world in the Realm of Monsters. Everything that led here, the loss of my mother, the betrayal of so many, the way Aric looked at me before he was ripped away, it's all still so fresh in my mind.

And it's just a weapon for my reckless magic.

The jaws of my wolf snarl before latching onto the thin skin of the creature carrying me off into the fiery skyline. My eyes close tightly, and it's then that power billows out of me in waves of magic I still don't fully understand. It's the most euphoric wave that's only a slight sensation of what my victim feels.

Which is total, relaxed euphoria.

A pleasant moan of contentment is the last thing I hear from my assailant of a monster fucking beast.

Before the bat releases me in its slackened jaw.

And I free fall.

Soul Kissed

***

The strength of the arms around me stops my teeth from rattling. The night blankets us in chilling, harsh winds, the opposite of the daylight hours that scorch my dry flesh. Torben holds me against his chest, and I stare out into the flames that grow like weeds from the cracks of the earth. The distance Latham put between us and the monsters far below the treetop is the only reprieve. The treetops here are mountainous. The trunks regal among the burning world that's crumbling around them.

Latham keeps watch though. He hasn't left my side for a single second. I don't know if either of them will ever again.

Latham's fiery, beastly form lies lazily on a thick branch, more catlike than hellhound, but he's majestic all the same. And for some reason . . . the creatures far below respect him.

Perhaps that's the honor that comes from being a son of Loki.

Or perhaps he's just more frightening than I give him credit for. They all are really. Torben, Latham, and Aric are men of Hell. Beasts that will kill a man simply for speaking wrongly to me. As they did with Kyvain.

But I've never thought of them like that. They're not

monsters . . . they're just *mine*.

And I should have protected what's mine the way they protected me.

Though Torben swipes back my hair with care and worry, I know he's thinking of his friend. Just like I am.

"He's okay. We'll get him back," Torben whispers quietly along my neck.

My eyes close hard, and I try not to think of it again. I block out the cruel glint in Kyvain's eyes. I refuse to imagine it all over again for the hundredth time.

But the sinking of my heart is a memory that plays on repeat over and over again with each second that slips by in the chaotic night of the Realm of Monsters.

Aric's gone.

And it's entirely my fucking fault.

I swallow down the tension in my throat and refuse to cry in Torben's arms. I won't be that girl.

I've lost too much, and I won't lose the strength I have and who I am.

"I don't—" My voice dips with a sob I bite back immediately. "I don't want to talk about it," I say dryly.

Latham peers back at me with gleaming eyes that remind

me of a Hell cat that I lost as well. And as for the mother I went into all of this for . . .

Tears stream down my face, and I can't stop them. I can't stop the silent emotions streaking down my cheeks.

"Don't promise me we'll get him back," I growl through clenched teeth. "Promise me we'll kill Kyvain for what he did."

Torben's big body tenses around me while Latham's gaze holds mine. A beat of uncertainty slips by in the screaming wind.

And then he whispers like words of love against my ear, "I promise."

Chapter Two

A Likable Guy

Aric

The laughter sputters from my lips as I hang before him. The hot trickle of blood running down my lips really puts a damper on the humor in my tone.

"You hit like a little school bitch at recess," I hiss between the pain rising up in my abdomen.

The prick, Kyvain, glares harder at me before doubling up his fist and once more using his new favorite punching bag: *me*. The breath knocks from my lungs as stars and spots dot my vision, and, still, I force myself to smile through the pain. Because all the agony in all the realms is worth it if the one woman I care about is safe away from this hell-hole.

She's free. She's safe.

I hope.

"Your mom teach you that swing, kid?" The groan in my throat comes out despite the hold I try to keep on it. "Try again. This time, actually aim," I add as a warm line of blood slides from my lower lip.

His curses run over my name as he mumbles under his breath like the cowardly fuck that he is.

Through the blur of my vision, I see him double his little baby fist once more. My body stiffens for the blow to come. My stomach tenses hard, my eyes clench closed, and I wait.

. . . shit, did I make him cry or something?

One of my eyelids cracks open. The woman who has owned my existence since the dawn of time tilts her sharp chin to look up at me where I hang on the dining room wall like a stuffed moose head.

"Hela, darling, how have you been?" I ask with a crooked smile and a cough I can't contain.

"I like you, Aric," she says with a glint in her eye like an evil witch about to offer me a date rape apple.

"I'm a likable guy. Just ask my new friend Kylie over there."

"Kyvain," he corrects sharply. The queen of hell and I both ignore the crying toddler in the room.

"I'm sending you on another trip." She clasps her hands quietly in front of her, and the sick, sinking feeling in my stomach starts up as it always does when she sends me somewhere.

Who will I capture for her? Who will I kill? Whose life will I ruin?

"I love trips," I say instead. "I could use a vacation." I blow out a breath as I twist in my restraints.

Her lips purse against her smile. "Good. Kyvain," she snaps and turns his way finally. "Release him. Get cleaned up and then the two of you are off."

With a grand sweeping of her cascading, black dress, she turns away from me and Kylie.

"Where to, my queen?" I ask with my heart pounding out of my chest at the idea of what destruction is sure to come.

She doesn't look back. For a moment, I don't think she'll grace me with an answer at all.

Her one-word reply is a cool breeze down the hall as it echoes back at me in her regal wake.

Soul Kissed

"*Muspelheim.*"

Chapter Three

Do Itttt

Rhys

Torben has always been the leader. The one who knows how everything works. He understands where to go and where to look. Except here, we just sit.

And do *noth-ing*.

There's no exit. There's no mystery key to turn into the sky. There's no mountain to leap from.

There's fuck all and fire in this realm.

And now there's us.

"Do you think he knows what you're doing to him?" Latham tilts his head as I stare into the monstrous bat's big black eyes. The dazed and foggy look he gives me is like a lovesick puppy.

Because he is. I've drugged him with enough of my magic that I'm starting to think he's found an addiction.

"Yes. I think he knows. The same way anyone would know if I stared into their eyes and made them feel orgasmically good without even touching them."

A deep coughing sputter lifts my attention to the man leaning back on our tree trunk, casually resting high up in the heavens like the warrior god that he is. And now . . . my warrior god is . . . is he blushing?

It's always the brutish men who are secretly the shiest.

Latham sits at the edge of the branches of trees in his now human form. He's perfectly dressed in a dark sweater for the chill of the evening night. The big star that resembles a moon of this realm halos around his lithe form, silhouetting him in darkness except for his shining eyes that glint back and forth between me and Torben.

I hold his mischievous gaze as a slow smile overtakes his handsome face.

"Do it," Latham hisses.

"Do what?" Torben grunts.

"Do ittttt," Latham urges once more, and I knew long before he ever said anything what he was thinking.

"Do what?!" Torben growls as his brows harden his face with confusion and anger.

I flick my attention away from the enormous bat that's laying one of its two heads in my lap and stare wickedly into the emerald sea of Torben's deep eyes. My magic stirs inside me, and it's such a conspiratorial feeling of what I'm about to do that it doesn't even feel sensual in this moment.

It feels taunting.

"Don't," Torben warns. His big hand lifts like he could block my sexy mind attack, but we both know he can't.

The bat flutters his big head, and then, with a wailing movement of his wings, he soars out into the night and away from the thunderous sound of Torben's empty threats.

Empty. That's exactly what they are.

So . . . I lock eyes with him once more, focus my intent, and . . .

He's on his feet. Leaves shake around me. Branches tremble beneath me. In three storming strides, his body collides into mine. My heart pounds as loudly as the thudding impact. Balance is lost, and the weight of his body

against mine knocks me right off the thick branch. The cool air hits my lungs in a gasp, and it's all a fearful blur.

Until I open my eyes. I stare suddenly up into the strangest mesmerizing look within the hooded gaze he holds on me. My arms are locked around his thick neck, and he holds me with one hand around my waist, melding me against his body as he hangs tight with his other hand to the branch above.

I'm reminded of Tarzan and Jane. I've never felt so suspended in my own emotions. Everything I feel and smell and think is Torben. Especially as those jade, hooded eyes lower to my lips, and ever so softly, my attacker presses the gentlest kiss there.

I breathe him in. Fear isn't a thought in my head anymore. It's just us.

And I suddenly wonder if he somehow used my own love magic against me.

"I told you not to use your power on me," he growls breathily against my mouth.

I press another slow kiss along his frown, his tongue flicking out to meet mine.

"I didn't," I whisper before he kisses me again. The tenderness he shows isn't something I'd ever expect from

13

him. But he gives it to me time and time again.

His eyes open just barely to meet mine.

"Then why do I feel like this, Rhys?"

Blooming tingles flood my flesh like a thousand nerves firing at once.

Because I feel it too.

And with that intense, consuming emotion filling every part of me, I finally understand just how much power I truly hold.

Enough to bring every man and monster to their knees.

Starting with Hela.

Chapter Four

Kylie

Aric

Even the way he walks is pretentious: like his arms are too big for his body and have to have their own force field when he struts.

"No hard feelings, right?" he says after a stream of comparing my intentional slaughtering of his life to the fuck hole of a position he has put me in now.

"Right," I agree casually. Because it's true. There are no hard feelings.

Because I'll get my lover back. And he'll die once again.

"No hard feelings," I tell him.

In the dehydrated desert of Muspelheim, the aridity alone could kill someone. The bats that creep out at dusk, those could swallow a man up in one bite.

Especially a little, puny alpha like Kylie here.

We pass a geyser. The white-hot stream of steam twirling out catches my eye, and the flickering image of Kylie tripping right into it plays on repeat in my mind.

"Ever been here?" he asks as he leads the way like he has spent summers here every year since he was a boy.

"Not for a long, long time."

"Shame Rhys couldn't have fallen into a different realm for us to chase her down in. Somewhere—" he slaps at a wild horsefly, and it neighs angrily as it flutters off. "Somewhere more tropical would have been nice."

I roll my eyes at his complete lack of a real personality. The real shame here is that the Goddess Moon actually mated this dense asshole to my sweet Rhys.

"You really felt a bond with Rhys?" The question spews out, and I regret the curiosity instantly.

His carving smile alone tells me how much he enjoys it though. He's fucking loving my thoughts of them together and I hate myself immensely for it.

Soul Kissed

"Felt like a rip of power right through my heart the second I laid eyes on her under the Dark Moon." There's a glassy-eyed stare as he looks off into the setting sunlight that I want to pound right out of his fucking skull.

I've never felt that power. I'll never feel that with Rhys. I wasn't chosen for her. I wasn't good enough for her in that sense.

I can only love her and hope it's enough.

I swallow hard, and the steel that strains my mouth shut is almost painful.

"When we fuck for the first time, that power in my soul will only intensify. She'll complete me in a way she won't ever understand." A chuckle shakes out of his arrogant mouth. "She always was a tempting piece of ass. Even for a freak like her."

With a flash of my fist, I fucking knock his cocky ass out.

Again.

Dammit!

I was doing so good this time too.

Chapter Five

Going . . . South

Latham

"The Southlands," Torben disgruntledly grunts as he leaps from the tree.

Rhys is right behind him and both of them storm passed me from where I sit seated in the dry dirt.

"And you've never explored there? You never thought an exit might reside in the one place no one wants to go?" Rhys stands impatiently, but Torben practically rushes to beat her to her feet.

"Because it's dangerous. No one goes there because the

Southlands are the dead man's land."

"We have to go. We have to at least try." She has said that over and over again, but what she really means is *we have to get Aric back.*

I agree. I want him back as badly as she does, but I know Aric better than her. He's not in danger even with Hela. He's too good at what he does. He's too smart, despite how stupid he acts. Hela might beat him, but she won't kill him.

And that's why I remain sitting against our trusty tree. Yep. I'm completely undisturbed by the idea of Aric talking in circles around Hela until she throws one of his weird, antique, limited edition butter dishes at his pretty face.

"Let me go," Torben says with finality.

Even I arch a brow at that. I've never been, but the southlands aren't called the dead man's land for nothing.

"No!" Rhys's long blonde hair swishes against her back as she looks from me to him and back again. "Tell him no!"

I consider her command, and as much as I want to give in to her every time she opens her cherry lips, I won't let her go. I won't let her risk her life for an idiot who's probably flouncing around Hela's castle in My Little Pony onesie jammies as we speak.

"He's right." The moment I speak, her frustration grows

with a stern line between pale, arched eyebrows, but ultimately, she waits for me to finish. "He should go. If there's an exit, he'll find it. And he'll come back for you."

You. Because three men of hell care about this beautiful woman more than we'll ever care about our own miserable lives. If I spend the rest of my days in this wasteland, it'll be no different than what I had before.

Except now I have her. And I won't let harm ever come to her.

Torben's nod is stern, and he gives her an assured look. Then he turns abruptly and heads south like all is settled, fine and dandy.

The tension in Rhys's brow alone tells me he's an idiot and absolutely nothing is settled. A heavy breath of air slips from my lips as I shake my head at him. He's terrible at this.

"Hey!" Rhys yells at his broad back as he saunters off into the night. She storms after him like a true goddess about to bring down her wrath.

I feign disinterest, but my gaze lifts entirely when I see her wrap her arms around his torso. She hugs him hard for so long, even I feel the pressure of emotions that has built up between them. I always feel it when she's close to one of

20

us. The affection seems to build and she can't contain it within herself. It feels heavenly.

She loves him.

And he's too much of a fool to tell her he loves her too.

Shit.

I shake away the thoughts creeping into my mind about my own confusing relationship with her and try to focus on the gnarly, two-headed bat that lies strangely in her spot. I didn't even think bats lay like this at all, but the creature won't leave her side now. Both of its enormous bobbleheads watch her with big black eyes as it waits for her to come back like it's her favorite lap puppy.

Thing gives me the creeps, and that's saying something.

My attention shifts, and I pick more intently at the bark of the dry twig in my hand as her boots scuff across the dirt. She sits quietly across from me, her bat pet settling itself with its heads in her lap when she crosses her legs.

She strokes the closest one absently as she stares off into the dark night. The creature makes a bizarre noise, and I can't help when my lip curls at its creepy happiness. It's obsessed with her. And the feel of her magic. It has been mesmerized by her since the moment it saw her.

Shit.

I'm the creepy bat pet.

I'm all but tripping over myself to get my head in her lap and coo for her attention. I followed her to the Realm of Monsters.

What the fuck has happened in my life?

My hand shoves hard through my hair, and I shake off the idea that I'm anything like the big-headed beast. It shows row after row of teeth, but it's not ferocious. It's fucking adorable. Her long fingers push back and forth across the beast, giving him all of her attention she can spare.

Damn. Why do I wish that was me right now?

I lower my gaze and pick at the bare twig a little more. She gives everything: She gives her affection. She gives her magic freely. I should let her have her time to herself. It's what she needs after everything that's happened.

The scent of honey drifts over me just a second before her arm brushes smoothly down mine. Side by side we sit, and it's impossible for me to not want to lean into her, to speak to her, to have her. She's intoxicating.

"He'll be fine, you know."

"I know." She sighs.

"I once saw him get eaten by a black wrath shark."

Soul Kissed

Her eyes widen with terror, and I realize immediately that that was the wrong way to start this reassuring story.

"He killed the beast from the inside out. I still have no idea how he did it," I add quickly. Her soft smile is gentle and sweet. Just like she is. I bump my shoulder into her like a boy with a crush he'll never be able to explain in words. "He'll be fine."

"I know," she says once more with more conviction than last time.

A thought forms in my mind, and I try to ignore it. Now's not the time. But I could distract her. I'm good at distracting. I'm so, so fucking good at it.

The dirty thought spins like a carousel over and over until I reach for her hand ever so subtly. She lets me. Her soft palm slides into mine, our fingers sliding together slowly in the most delicious way. Those thoughts are thrusting in harder now. Pounding in with demanding, distracting abilities.

Soft blonde hair falls across my shoulder. Her head rests there as her big eyes close with a line of worry etching her brows.

My lips press tenderly to her temple, and I breathe her in as I speak.

23

"Every single thing is going to work out, Rhys. We'll never let anything happen to you," I whisper.

Her lashes lift, and when our gazes meet, there's no longer space between us.

Only heated glances and yearning emotions fill the space. Her energy is magnetic. Delicious. Something I'll feel deep down in my chest every time I simly look at her.

With a tilt of her chin, she brushes her lips across mine. I'd wanted to kiss her. To distract her. And here she is taking all that from me. And giving it right back.

Her tongue flicks across mine, parting my lips with ease, and I'm not even sure this was my idea in the first place now. Perhaps the Goddess of Love has mind control abilities too. If that's true, I never want to think for myself for the rest of my damn life.

I sink into the push and pull of her caresses. Her kiss alone is consuming, demanding me to grip her soft locks and pull her closer for more. But more isn't enough. And apparently, she feels the same way.

Her thighs shift over my lap, and soon, she's straddled across my hips, holding me with both hands the way I'm holding her. Neither of us seem to ever want to let go. Her forceful fingers pull painfully against the roots of my hair, and still I only groan to feel her deeper. Dry dirt and dust cling to the tattered fabric my fingers twist into. I pull away the cloth, and it's tossed aside, forgotten the moment it's gone. Somehow, every scrap of material separating her smooth curves from my touch is discarded in the same way. My shirt's gone, and I don't even know when we did away with it either. Because the heat of our bodies is burning up our thoughts. Only a single thing is on our minds.

Feeling her and the energy she expels without even trying, is a light show. It's fireworks and sparks.

It's magic.

Her hips lift, and her wetness slides down my shaft, never giving me the closeness I truly want but teasing me with what's just out of reach.

She feels so good. My hands tremble from the power within her.

I clench my fists and focus on her taste. A needy growl reverberates from my lips to hers, and her smile is a bright and shining thing as she stares down on me with stars in her eyes.

Sparkling only at me.

With a light press of her hand around the back of my neck, she pulls me closer, her lips hovering over mine. She holds me. She controls me. She owns me. Then she sinks down. My mouth gasps with every inch, feeling her glide down my cock, gripping and greedy as she takes everything I have to give like it has always been hers.

Maybe it has.

"Fuck," I hiss. "Fuck, I love you, Rhys," I vow.

And then, with her hand still wrapped around me, our bodies as close as two lifelong lovers, realization falls. I stare up at my goddess. Her eyes shine with a dampness I hadn't noticed before. *Did I ruin it? Why did I say that? Why did I say that right now?*

"I love you too," she whispers right back on a shaking exhale that drives shivers all down my arms.

And that's exactly how each passing second feels as we lose ourselves within ourselves. It's hours of uneven breaths, inhales we can't catch or keep or even want. All that I feel and all that I want is her. The shivers she sends racing through me over and over again are an addiction I can't stop chasing as I drive my hips up to meet hers, burying myself as deep as she'll let me until I can't fucking take it anymore.

A hard shudder consumes me. It tenses every muscle and steals away every breath as I tip my head up to her and slam my lips to hers as the trembling pressure between us explodes. Stars rain down behind my eyes, and it only brightens with new pounding waves of release when I feel her tighten around my cock, nails dragging across my back as she presses me harder to her damp breasts. Not a single breeze of the dry desert can separate us.

Nothing ever will. I swear it.

I gaze up at her hooded, starry eyes. I'll keep her forever. I'll love her forever. I fucking vow it.

All those pretty thoughts are ripped away all too fast though.

Dirt kicks across my thighs, raining rock and dust all across our sweat-dampened bodies. Torben's groan of pain is the last thing I hear before I stare up into the most demonic black eyes.

We are not alone.

Chapter Six

The Humnih

Rhys

Torben's knees hit the ground in a puff of dust while Latham wastes no time at all on shock and awe. With a twist of his wrist, his magic flashes clothes across my body as well as his. They hug me perfectly as if his simple touch alone knows every detail of my skin. He's standing with a blazing sword lighting up the night in less than half a second.

"Let him go," he shouts at the . . . woman. She's a woman, I think.

Her long black hair hangs down her bare, graying shoulders in waves of silk. Sharp nails elongate her already boney

fingers. Her dress is rags of dirty fabric that seem unimportant in her life. She's larger than life and more terrifying than anything I've yet seen here.

Especially when her inky lips part with a voice that echoes like static cutting up a radio.

"Give us the girl, and I'll give you the male," she says, every word vibrating through the air harshly.

"Fuck you." Latham swings his blade out in one fluid move, but without even touching him, she lifts her hand and sends out unseen power. It slams into his chest, and with a hard thump, he hits the dirt at my side.

I watch her. Tension snaps through my body to lash out at her, but something tells me to wait. A nagging sensation at the back of my mind pulls at me to wait. Not to harm her. She's alone, but she said *give us the girl*. Who is *us*?

"Who are you?" I ask carefully, my fists tightening at my sides despite my mind's constant déjà vu that haunts my intuition.

She has Torben! She has the man I care about, and my wolf deep inside simply snoozes away without a single worry.

What is happening right now?

"I am Venus. I am speaker of the Humnih." Her large head bows low as she speaks to me.

Huh. She hadn't done that to Latham. As if thinking the same thing, he grunts at my side, his fiery glare still held on the monstrous woman.

Torben's messy, dark hair shifts around his face as he discreetly peers up at me. He hasn't said one word. He isn't in pain . . . As a matter of fact, the rope binding his wrists in front of him seems feeble in comparison to the strength I know the god possesses.

"What do you want with me?" I tilt my head at her, and the woman's eyes light up with interest as she looks down on me like I'm a tiny ruby at her feet.

"We want peace," she whispers, her voice echoing like wind whipping around my ears.

"Peace?" Skepticism slips in, but once more, my wolf acts as my mind's eye: She's not a danger to me.

I hope.

"Let me take you to my people. The Humnih have been waiting far too long for our messiah."

Messiah?

Shit, that's not right, I don't think . . .

***

Latham, though his hands are bound and though he put up

a hell of an argument about it, walks at my side. He guards me with everything he has. Even if the woman leading us could whomp his ass to the ground all over again if she wanted.

"Why are we doing this?" Latham murmurs after an hour of dense silence.

"Because she knows something we don't," Torben says, his own hands held loosely in their bindings in front of him.

"She's going to kill us," Latham urges.

"I won't," Venus tells him.

But he shakes his head like he'll never believe the monstrous woman.

"Right. Thanks for the reassurance. I'll sleep peacefully now." He says it less dramatically and more cordially than Aric would have, but it still stings the thought through my head.

Part of me agrees with his apprehension. Part of me wants to ask about Aric. And part of me wants exactly what this stranger wants: peace.

I've never had that. Not in my pack. Not with my mother. Not now or ever.

Maybe that's the mysterious sensation my wolf keeps

sending out to me.

Or maybe I'm just crazy.

The screams of creatures continue to scar the night as we trail out into the darkness. A swooping overhead tells me my favorite bat is following. So many unseen things are lurking all around us. Perhaps to the other monsters of this world, we are the threat.

I stare up at the woman's long, shining black hair. Everything about her is covered in dirt just like the three of us. Except her hair. It's very cared for. It's long and glossy and smoothly brushed.

It's what sticks out most when a fire blazes up in yellows and reds into the skyline up ahead. And more women stand waiting at the fireside. The three of them have the same trait. Long hair down to their waists and knees. That's all I can make out about the silhouettes ahead.

I can't explain why their image is so comforting.

Until . . .

A tiny speck of a creature starts darting down the hill toward us. I see it zip through the thin terrain, and the air in my lungs catches hard. *What is it? Why did they send it down to us? Why did I trust this strange woman so freely?*

It was a mistake.

32

Soul Kissed

Sometimes the smallest things, the things so tiny you could overlook them, they're the deadliest. Just like me.

I search my emotions and my thoughts for the feel of the beast that resides within me. Except my wolf is a stubborn cunt sometimes. Because she once more is unfazed by a monster rushing through the night.

Headed straight for us.

"Latham," I whisper in warning to the man so close, he's brushing against my side.

His arm tenses with power, and though he's bound and though I'm free, I know I can count on him. Always.

But then I see it. A furry, little monster is running on four paws down to us. Not us. Me! And it's not a creature at all. It isn't a monster or a death threat.

I mean. It is.

Kind of.

It totally is.

With a swoop of its black tail and a rush of happiness flooding through me, it leaps.

And Latham tackles the tiny cat to the dust with no hands to help his fall. He flattens over the tiny house cat like a mega fly swatter slamming down on a speck of a pest.

"What the fuck, Latham!" I shove him off, and his muted groan is the last thing I hear before a quiet meow reassures everything in me. "Oh, Loki," I coo, scooping him up and rubbing my head against his. "Sweet boy, you're okay."

"Fucking. House cat." Latham's grunting curses are unheard over the sound of content purring in my ears.

"How did he get here?" I rush after the woman ahead of us to ask once more a bit louder.

Even as another familiar beast stands tall on enormous paws ahead of us.

"The hell dog," I whisper. The memory of the kind beast standing guard outside of the literal gates of Hell is fresh in my mind.

"The Humnih are peace bringers. We take in the abused. We bring them here to our realm. But our realm . . ." Venus looks out over the blackness of the night as if she can see the ruin of it all too clearly. "It hasn't been the same in a long, long time."

"The Realm of Monsters wasn't always a hell-hole," Torben tells me as we come into the circle of women and their fire.

"Silence, male!" The Humnih woman commands, her lip curling back at the very sight of the two men on either side

of me.

"You brought them here, Messiah?" the tallest of the three woman asks, her hair done in long sweeping braids that nearly touch her ankles.

"Um. Yes. Torben and Latham and I came into this realm to escape Hela and the Elfie—elf king," I say, correcting his name fast before anyone can notice.

"The elf king." The woman on the left spits, literally spits his name. "He is unwelcome in Muspelheim."

"Yes!" The tall woman agrees with hate seething through her inky teeth.

"Another time, sisters," the leader of the three says. With a sweep of her hand, she reveals a shelter carved into the stony wall just behind them, and beneath the canopy of the rock, dozens of women sit cross-legged and silent.

They look out to us. Black, shining eyes stare intently at one thing: me.

"Where—where are the men?" I ask suddenly.

"Men," the woman on the left repeats and once more spits at the dry ground.

Wow. I need to choose better discussion topics, clearly.

"The Humnih are women, Young Messiah," The leader

says in the eerie static tone of theirs. "Men are not a necessary part of life."

"Mmm," the woman on the right agrees with another nod.

"They're . . . fun. Sometimes," the leader says while the other two women roll their eyes hard. "But they're a disaster to clean up after. They forget—*everything*. Can't remember a day's topic to save their lives. Their brains . . . tiny, little things. Like raisins."

Torben coughs hard at my side, sounding as though he might choke on the insult alone, but ultimately, he says nothing.

A high screech of an announcement calls out just before my favorite two-headed bat swoops down. He walks strangely on his strong back legs like a sort of dragon, using his upper wings as talons as he careens over to my side. The monster and the cat assess one another for a long moment, but there's an unspoken peace here beneath the eyes of the Humnih. They were both brought to this realm by these proud and protective women. Where was the bat before he came here? Was his life like mine? Worse. It was probably much worse.

But mostly, I can't help but wonder how much love and compassion it must take for these women to risk their lives for others. I mean, not men, but I can see they've been hurt by men in the past. They know the destruction someone like the elven king can bring.

They won't risk that danger here in their realm. Not again.

And I can understand that.

"Tell us, Messiah, what are your plans for the Realm of the Living?"

My brows lift, naturally. "We plan to return." Once I get Aric back, all I want is to disappear into California. I'll live away from my pack. Away from the ones who don't understand me. And we'll be safe. Happy. Normal.

Normal. That's the goal in life, isn't it?

After everything, after losing my mother, it's all I want.

"And how will you help the afflicted?" the leader asks with a serious, inquisitive gaze.

. . . the afflicted? I—I think I was the afflicted . . .

Who's the newly afflicted?

"The afflicted?"

The woman on the left with the shortest temper and the shortest amount of patience, it seems, speaks up. "The Hell Sufferers. The Ragnarok Reamers. The End of Days Doers."

My mind churns with all of those titles, and something seems very, very off.

"The End of Days?" Latham asks on a steady tone that I feel is teetering with every ounce of information I know he's collecting, organizing, and storing in that constant mind of his.

The three women don't acknowledge the man who spoke but instead inform me.

"The End of Days is upon them. The Realm of the Living is the first strike. Hela and her . . . *lover* have taken the first step. They've brought their Hell to Earth. And our realms outside of yours will be next."

My gaze stares straight ahead, but I see nothing. My thoughts have turned in on themselves, and the spiking nerves of my wolf are spiraling the images of the end of the world all through my head.

The end of the world. That's what Hela wanted all along. I thought my mother had been taken from my life as a cruel game to be played on not only me but the woman who made her lover love her. My mother, the Goddess of Love, gave me her magic. She unfortunately gave me the inherited vendetta the Queen of Hell has always had for my mother. It was passed on to me.

But revenge wasn't Hela's motive. It was just a pretty bonus on top.

"Why me?" I ask finally when the answers never add up.

The leader tilts her head at me as if in pity as well as confusion. No one speaks for a long moment. It passes by in cold silence that flits across my arms in lifted hairs that chill me to the bone.

"Because you're Love," Torben says in a rumbling softness.

The echoes of my mother's voice whisper through my mind: You are Love.

Not loved. *Love.*

I don't know why my heart stings to realize that correction of my memories.

"By extracting the Goddess of Love from the Realm of the Living. You expelled your magic freely. Even when you weren't aware. And now that love is gone. The balance is unstable in your world," Latham says, his tied hands reaching out and skimming along my numbed fingers. I can't hold his hand. I can't process enough of my surroundings when my mind is so filled with all of these scrambled facts and emotions.

I stagger away from him and his ghostly touch.

"Did you know?" I utter on barely a breath of a voice.

"No!" Latham and Torben both confess, but Torben's deep admission continues. "I only knew you were important to Hela. I didn't know why."

"We—I wish we never had taken you." Latham's tone drowns off into the night, but the pain in his tone rings out.

I blink at that. I think about the bleak life I had before. The daily ins and outs of being the pack outcast. Of being Kyvain's punching bag. And eventually . . . his whore.

They're wrong for thinking that. These men, they have no idea what they mean to me.

"No!" I swallow that down hard. All the love they've shown me in the mere moments we've been together is more love than I've felt in my entire life.

I am Love.

But I've never felt it.

Until them.

"No," I whisper more gently, my eyes closing hard to the prickling tears hiding behind my lashes. I shake it all off and face the Humnih leader once more. "We want to save them, the Realm of the Living."

"Of course," she replies.

Soul Kissed

But how? I don't say that for fear of losing this proud woman's respect.

"We don't know how to get out of this realm and into another. We're missing another member of our . . . pack."

Latham's brows lift, and a smile like the golden sun lights up his eyes.

A pack. We're a whole ass pack of misfits. And I fucking love every part of it.

"Where—" The woman's vibrant voice is cut abruptly when her gaze lifts to the horizon, the darkness capturing in her inky eyes. "Someone is here."

My spine stiffens at the sound of her concern, but I barely have time to turn around when a war cry sounds. I always thought an attack would be like a knife blade to the heart. A scream of vengeance and a cry for justice. This . . . this isn't any of that.

"You stupid fuckin' whore!" Kyvain's voice alone splinters through my soul. A lifetime of hate lies there, and it shatters out in rage at the memory of what he has done to me but also to Aric. His arm's wrapped around my throat, and he's hauling me back.

Anger shouts out from a group of Humnih but also from the sounds of aggression from the men bound in rope at my sides. Even the screech of a wicked bat and a hiss of a loyal cat resound all around me.

But my head slamming back into his is the final crack of noise that cuts off his attack. Torben's stomping boots flurry the dirt around the asshole on the ground. Kyvain covers his nose, blood dripping through his fingers as sharp, snapping teeth lash out from his human jaws. Talons rip through his nails, and his beast howls for the final transformation.

Then a dirty black boot slams into Kyvain's face, halting the howls and promises of more to come in a single instant.

"Fucker loves to hear himself talk, doesn't he?" The most beautiful dragon shifter stands carelessly above my attacker, and my heart lifts at the mere sight of him.

"Aric!" His body is against mine before the jagged breath can even reach my lungs. I wrap him up in my arms, and the feel of his warmth searing into me is comfort I've never felt before.

Holding the one person I've thought of every second of the day is pure warmth to my soul. It's a mixture of calming and chaotic emotions that run rapid through my chest.

I never want to let him go.

"Fuck, Love. I'll let this asshole capture me all the time if you promise to hug me like this," his humor whispers against my messy hair, but the pressure of his hands against my back and the cutting emotion in his voice tells me he isn't amused at all.

He's relieved.

And all I want is to soak into that feeling of our emotions settling like quiet rain after a hurricane. He feels good. His body melding into mine feels like I can sense the magic I give to everyone else. My magic is different when I'm with them. It's stronger.

"You—you love him? You love all of them?" The woman, Venus, asks with uncertainty dripping down her words.

I pull back from Aric ever so slowly, taking in the shine of his deep yes. They seem so much more vibrant than I remember: A fiery golden brown. I never want to forget the light creases along the outer corner of his beautiful eyes ever again.

"I do. I love them." I lift my gaze to Torben and the seriousness of his features is hard and cutting as it always is. Except he looks terrified. More afraid than I've ever seen him in his entire life.

All because a woman admitted she loved him.

Should I not? Should I not have said that?

No. I won't hide the most important words from the most important people in my life. I love them. Even if Torben doesn't know how to process that at all. I love him anyway.

He turns away abruptly and meets the leader's studious stare.

"They're protective of the Messiah," the woman with the long braids whispers, and dozens of the others murmur quiet words between themselves that I can't hear.

"She's protective of them as well," Venus says, and everyone nods.

"I'd never considered having one male, much less three." The leader smirks as her friend curls her lips in disgust.

"Seems like a lot of work," one of them adds.

"You and your friends, we will take you to the Realm of the Living. We will take this male as a bargaining chip as well." The leader picks Kyvain's limp body up from the dirt like he's a used Band-Aid she doesn't truly want to touch.

I don't think Kyvain will be much of a bargaining chip for Hela. I don't think he'll matter much at all.

But I don't care, in the grand scheme of things.

Because Hell has come to Earth. And I'm the one person everyone suddenly needs.

Chapter Seven

Where It All Started

Rhys

The Humnih gather, standing tall like a forest all around my meager frame. Even Torben stares up at the giantess women with a bit of awe in the depths of his eyes. They gather with unspoken orders, their hands sliding within one another, creating links of strength with their arms alone. It happens in a matter of seconds, but I'm suddenly aware that the four of us and Kyvain's now bound body are at the center of their circle.

"What are they doing?" Latham rasps on the quietest of tones.

"Shh," Torben tells him.

It doesn't silence Latham's interest though. It only sets him off into a calculating frenzy as he tries to understand the sudden static noise that twirls round and round through the midnight air. A chant. A plea. A begging of words spoken in that eerie tone of theirs calls out to be heard . . .

But by whom?

Light moves between their interlocked hands like an electric-charged wind, binding them together in an unbreakable chain of magic. It sways in tune with the chants of words I can't understand but can feel down to my very bones. It's a feeling of power. It grows and grows. The wind blurs faster and faster. The magic, the words, the colors turn chaotic and demanding.

It all becomes too much.

Then it bursts.

I'm thrown back into someone. I collide into their chest without warning. They hold me close, but the light of star showers is all I can see. The colors fall all around me, blazing by with heat and force. Another set of hands clasps ahold of my trembling fingers, and it doesn't take long for me to realize they're all around me. Torben holds me from behind. The long fingers gripping my hand in theirs are

definitely Aric's. And the calming brush of a thumb pushing back and forth over my knuckles is the sweetest man I've ever met.

Amid the sky falling in on us, we still manage to find one another.

We always will.

My feet slam into solid ground in the next instant. A harsh breath falls from my lips, and I can't stop the next one and the next one from coming as I take in the fiery colors of the world around us.

I thought the Realm of Monsters looked like Hell. I was so fucking wrong.

The cottages that were my neighborhood for as long as I can remember are nothing more than smoking rubble. The flames of their wreckage have long since fizzled out, but the embers among the broken windows and charred framework burn with heat that licks across my flesh as I walk aimlessly past one small house after another. It's all such a mess, I can't even tell which one was once the home I used to hide away in. One of these piles of ashy remains was the only thing that kept my tormentors out. It allowed me to just breathe freely. To be myself.

And I guess that's why it hurts like a knife to the stomach

to see my pack and home in just despair.

The crunch of gravel beneath my feet can be felt more than it's heard. The shift of debris hinders my steps as I search the fiery horizon. An army of beautiful warrior women follow my lead, as do the hellish men and eerie creatures I've come to love. No one questions me. They simply follow while I take in the horrors of what was my past.

Town square is just ahead, and a small crowd flocks around the gazebo where once upon a time, beautiful weddings and happy birthdays were celebrated beneath it. The wood of the structure is cracked and charred. Only a jagged half of it stands tall with its peak still intact and centering the stunted silhouette of Dark Moon Academy just behind it.

Loki and a gathering of light elves stand strangely at the edge.

"Is this your doing?" Latham storms right up to his father.

"What? No. Not at all. Just came to see what all the fuss was about." Loki lifts his hands innocently, and it takes Latham and Aric several moments before finally nodding and tossing something to the ground like it's an old trash bin.

Kyvain's body slams to the dirt, and he remains unmoving.

My thoughts are so lost in it all that I don't recognize the

sound of her gasping voice until I'm at her feet where she hangs tied up by just her bruised and bloodied wrists. The air in my lungs seeps out in a desperate breath as I run to her battered body at the center of the gawking crowd.

Bea. Her head lolls to the side as tear-dampened lashes flutter aimlessly.

"*Please*," she begs on a dry whisper.

And no one, not one single member of this pathetic, cruel excuse of a pack, answers her. With harsh and jarring movements, I shove my way to the front.

"Move!" I growl at the few stragglers still lingering beneath the strange alter of a platform her small body is strung up on.

My fingers are fumbling when I finally reach her. Unsteady boots teeter on the edge of the narrow stone block her bare feet barely brush against. I stretch to pull at the gold chain linking around her red wrists high above her head. The metal stings strangely against my flesh, but I refuse to acknowledge the pain when my friend is enduring so much. I put all of my might into tearing at the ember flecks that burn off of the enchanted metal. Singed fingertips throb, gasps fall from my trembling lips, and still I will not let her go.

"Rhys, Rhys, stop." Strong hands grip my hips, fingers tensing into my skin with determination as I cling on to the golden chains for as long as I can. "You can't save her! You can't save her!" Aric's screams are lost against my neck, his lithe body melding to mine, his hold on me so tight that it hurts as I thrash against him.

He knows I won't stop though. I can tell he knows because he releases me with reluctant hands sliding around my arms as I fling myself forward once more. Power tears angrily through my viens and I grip the metal around her wrists once more. I pull so hard a cracking along my back teeth sounds but I can't stop.

I refuse to.

The burn of the metal numbs my fingers until I lose my grip. My body stumbles against her own. I don't hold onto her to save myself. Not for one second do I consider causing an ounce more of pain just to help myself.

I fall hard. My hands hit the rubble and concrete with stinging impact that reminds me that the numbness is only temporary.

I lie on the ground feeling useless and defenseless in protecting and aiding my friend. Aric lifts me slowly, helping me stand and holding me loosely in a consoling way that I can barely feel.

Torben's strength is fluid, and he leaps up onto the small block with ease. His fingers are nimble and quick as he fists the glowing chain with both hands. A moment of awe calms through my heart at how easily he takes care of any problem that crosses his path.

Except . . .

"Mother fucking goddess of Hell!" his roar is raw and ragged when he shoves away from the binds, and with a weighted thud, he lands on his feet back at my side. A tense line parts his brows, and he can't seem to look at me where I stand immobilized in Aric's arms. "Hela's magic can't be tampered with," he grunts.

My gaze holds on the light inhale and exhale of Bea's breaths. She's alive. But barely.

And once again, this mess is entirely my fucking fault.

And everything in me snaps. I tear away from the warmth of Aric's embrace, and I'm turning on the crowd of followers I'd forgotten were even there. There are more of us now. It isn't just me against the world. It's Hell cats and beasts and members of my pack and warrior women of a monstrous realm, and of course, three godlike men of Hell who have been by my side from the very start . . .

"What the literal hell is happening here?" A wetness clings to my lashes, and I can feel my lifelong friend just behind me even if I can't bear to look at her for another moment. "How—how did this happen?" I whisper through my teeth, and I can't contain the emotion and the rage that's twirling inside me.

Latham eyes his father once more, but his glare is cut short.

"Happened after the Dark Moon," a man answers lazily.

I lift my eyes to the shirtless elder. His hair is more gray than brown, but I recognize him. He lived just two houses down from mine.

"What happened?"

"Just after the Dark Moon, people here started to change. Fights were being broken up between siblings, mothers and children, and everyone in between. Some of us left the pack all together. But . . ."

He glances to the dozens of others standing nearby.

"But what?" Latham urges both gently and impatiently.

"The violence was the same in the city. Like the whole world went crazy overnight."

My attention flicks to Venus, her height towering over the others as she nods in understanding.

Soul Kissed

There is no love left in the world . . . is that true? My mother left me here to keep me from the cruel leaders of hell. Did she know the effect I'd have on the world I lived in? Or is this one of Hela's cruel games?

Just then, a low grunt and a curse hums quietly. Kyvain's body shifts, and with his foot, he shoves himself to roll onto his back. His bloody face stares up at the morning-kissed sky. Bloodshot eyes find mine. His dry lips part as he glares at me.

"S—" Latham's boot comes down hard and fast across Kyvain's face. His head jars, and there's instant silence, followed by whatever shitty thing this man was going to spew at me.

Damn. Where were these hellish guys all through high school and college when I needed them?

"Thanks," I whisper, and Latham just nods softly, a sort of *it was nothing* kind of gesture.

"This is Hela's doing," I say under my breath. "She's here somewhere. I know it. And I'm going to find her."

"No," Torben shakes his head, his hard, calculating gaze scanning the fighting all around us. "She'd never come here. She sent us here to get you. She'd never leave the comforts of Hell to come to a place like Earth,"

Wow. Our realm really is a shit hole, huh.

"Let's scour the area. I think you just being here will slowly bring everyone back to normal." Torben looks out at the fire and smoke of the world that's literally burning to the ground, and I notice the wince that flutters through his left eye.

"Right," Latham nods. Aric nods with his friends as well, but it's more of an uncertain and uncommitted agreement.

"We will help the injured for now," Venus says, and I note that her high, electric voice is now flat and normal here in the Realm of the Living. The dozens of warrior women head out and begin picking up large men from the ground as if they're nothing more than a small Coach bag to swing over their shoulders.

I want to hold her up, take the weight of her body off of the harsh magic of her chains. I have to stop all of this though. I can only save her if I stop the chaos.

I stumble away from Bea, and my heart hurts to turn my back on her. I'll make this right. I'll fix it all.

Somehow.

Kyvain's limp body is left behind. Honestly, he can't be any worse off than he is with us kicking him in his obnoxious face every few hours. Needless to say, I don't think of him once after we walk away.

A sharp hiss stings the air, and my protective Hell cat comes closer to my side when a man with a bent road sign swings out close to me just to pummel another man to the dirt.

"That's what you get for saying hi to my wife every morning!" he roars as he brings the street sign down once more with a clanging bang.

"I was your mail carrier, Jim. I said hello to *everyone*," the bloody-faced man explains.

Aric's big hand wraps around the metal post, and he jerks the makeshift weapon away from Jim. It's tossed to the ground, and Jim sets his blazing sights on my dragon instantly for interrupting him.

"That's enough," Aric says calmly.

But it's not *enough*. Every muscle beneath the man's dirty white shirt tenses as he turns fully to the three men of Hell who surround me.

But this is my fight. All of this is.

And I have to fix it. Now.

I push past Latham and Torben, and I make my way to the very front to look up at the crazed man who just beat a postal worker for no damn reason.

How the fuck do I fix this?

I think about the power inside of me. I even lift my hand and place it gently against his wrist. Anxiety for what I've caused swirls through my chest. Pain and guilt run rampant, and it all just clouds my thoughts as well as my magic. I just keep trying though. Everything's going to be okay. It will be. It has to be.

A big hand shoves to my chest. The suddenness of it throws me off balance and into Torben as Jim stares at me like I'm the biggest idiot he's ever had to look at.

"Take your weird little girlfriend and get the hell outta my sight!"

Latham's entire posture changes as he squares his shoulders and takes a solid step closer to the man. Aric picks up the battered road sign from the dirt, and everything feels even more out of control and chaotic.

"Stop! Stop it!" I grab Latham's arm and pull the metal sign from Aric's grip before these two Hell shifters beat this man to death with a *Lover's Lane* street sign. "We're supposed to be helping!" I shove my hands through my hair and storm off away from the mess of this screwed-up place.

Soul Kissed

I need to calm down. I need to channel my magic.

Through the throng of screaming and fighting and fire, I find myself face to face with the shattered glass door of Dark Moon Community College. It has been ransacked. A chair and forgotten papers lie in the empty hallway. I step through the jagged glass frame, and a bitter smile touches my lips. It's ridiculous that this shitty building is still intact. It has seen so much brutality and endured the worst of it.

And it's still standing.

Just like me, I guess.

I've failed time and time again. Still I keep going.

And for what? To come right back to the misery I started in?

I'm drawn to the open door to the right. It's so quiet here, my slow footfalls squeak across the old floors. I grew up in these halls and classrooms thinking I lived in hell. And now I really do.

A sigh that has been stuck in my lungs for years shakes over my lips, and I let my legs give out as I slide down the cold white wall. My boot kicks the door, and its hinges cry as it slides nearly shut.

You are loved.

Her voice rings in my ears over and over. It haunts me the same as it did all my life. Except now my stomach feels sick to think of her memory.

You are loved.

"What a fucking joke," I whisper to myself.

The squeal of old hinges sounds once more, and my attention lifts to the godlike man staring down on me. Torben's strength flexes even as he simply holds the frail wooden door in his enormous hand.

He'll break it if he pushes too hard, and we both know it.

"*Rhys.*" He says my name like a question and a heartbreak all at the same time.

It sounds like it hurts him to say my name with so much compassion.

"You're afraid of loving me." I turn on him. I accuse him quickly just to avoid the thousands of messy problems and thoughts waiting at the back of my mind.

His golden-brown eyebrows lift high, his lips parting as if he has already prepared a defense for this conversation.

"Not at all," he says swiftly.

Assuredly. Damn, he's always so fucking confident, isn't he?

And I'm left speechless.

"Oh."

A soft smile, a charming smile like kindness and alluring sexuality, pulls at his lips. He leans into the wall, letting his big body slide down right next to mine. His head slides back against the painted cylinder blocks, and I can tell he'd much rather think about this meager little problem in our lives than the literal Hell on Earth that awaits us just outside of these classroom windows.

"I'm not afraid of loving you, Rhys."

"I saw your face when I said it. I see the look in your eyes every time affection accidently slips between us. You're either afraid, or . . ." Realization and pain strike through my heart all at once.

Oh.

Oh my god, I'm such an idiot.

Torben . . . isn't afraid of loving me . . . he just doesn't feel that way at all.

"I'm so stupid." The words breathe out, and my legs shake as I try to stand.

Except a large hand slides over mine, and I'm pulled back down. I jostle into his side, my fingers splaying over his chest as I stare sadly up at the most beautiful warrior-like man I've ever had the misfortune of falling in love with.

"I'm sorry," I whisper as I turn away, but he holds me against him.

"Rhys! I'm not afraid of loving you! I—I don't deserve it! I—I—fuck." His head hits the wall once more, but this time with a harder thud. "I've never . . . had anyone love me before. It's . . . it feels twisted. I feel guilty for taking your love when I don't deserve it! I feel like a fake for making you love me! And . . . I feel completely weak every time I realize how fucking hard I fell in love with you . . ."

The hurt in the core of my chest stirs, but it turns into something more than sadness. It turns into pity. I look up at him with tragic, big eyes, and for the first time, I understand how much Hela completely wrecked this man.

He doesn't think he's worthy of love?

My arms fling around him fast and hard, and though I can't fully hold him, I meld him against myself anyway. I wish I could make him see himself the way I do. I wish I could heal him. But that'll take time. All I can do for now is love him.

Entirely.

The press of my lips against his is bruising. Our breaths

collide between us before our tongues ever do. Possessive hands thrust through my hair, and he pulls hard at the roots as I straddle over his big thighs. I'm pulsing with emotion. The beat of my heart is felt through every inch of me from the simple feel of his body brushing against mine.

Strong hips lift and tease against my core, and a hum of desire slips from my lips before he devours it whole. My magic sparks. It lights up from his touch alone.

This is it! This is exactly what I needed to channel the power inside me.

"Excuse me?!" A cutting voice slices through the heavy tension and silence. "If you two haven't noticed, the entire fucking world is on fire right now!" We both pull back ever so slightly to give Aric's rant a bit of our heated attention. "You really think right now is a good time for a school make out session?"

Latham's smirk appears as he pushes open the classroom door a little more.

Torben doesn't move an inch. He certainly doesn't release his firm hold on my hair.

"Ragnarök has come," Torben tells them in a deliciously gravelly voice. His grip on my hair turns to a caress as he twirls the ends of my locks with a sweet, dazed look in his hooded eyes. "It's the end of days. Is there somewhere else you'd rather spend your final days on Earth?"

Aric's mouth tenses, his brow lifting as he tilts his head this way and that. "I guess I hadn't thought of it like that . . ." He peers over at Latham, and the two of them share an unspoken decision. Less than a split second slips by before both of them reach for their jeans and start unbuttoning.

Aric kicks off his pants and is scrambling across the room in no time.

It's unknown to them but very known to me, that they strengthen my power. Every shared look, every brief touch, every heated kiss, it storms power through me.

And we fucking need that power right now.

What was heavy on my mind just moments ago is eased and calmed when Latham's lips press softly against my neck. Warm, steady palms slide down my shoulders, my arms, my hips, and then they're pushing across my ribs with so much tenderness, tears sting against the backs of my eyes. I never once felt love within the walls of this place.

And now . . . *I'm surrounded by it.*

My jeans are shoved down, and I shimmy them off in a hurry.

I let my lashes close before I can give myself time to think.

Soul Kissed

I fall into the feel of their needy hands against my body. Shivers race across my stomach as big hands spread across my ribs and over my breasts. My nipples peak as rough palms lightly tease against sensitive flesh. Warm breaths kiss my neck, my lips, my breasts.

I rock my hips, and Torben shifts in rhythm beneath me. His thickness hardens beneath me. Too many layers separate his body from mine though. My hands lift to unbutton his jeans as well. Except controlling hands lift me slightly. My lashes flutter, but I refuse to look out at this world again. I refuse to leave the nirvana that these beautiful men have given me.

I have to focus. I have to let the waves build. I need them right now. My heart as well as my magic needs them.

A smooth shaft slides over my sex, and the gasp against my lips is silenced with a kiss. Their tongue meets mine just as someone else kisses their way up my throat. And someone else teases against my opening.

And then slides firmly in all at once. Aric's groan rumbles over my spine as his messy hair skims across my flesh there.

"Fucking greedy dragon," Latham murmurs against my ear.

Torben's laughter is quieted when he kisses me next, this time slower. His intimate kiss is a claim against my heart.

It's sweet and endearing.

And absolutely nothing like how Aric fucks me.

Rapid thrusts meet me from behind, and I have to pull back from Torben as a moan tears from my throat. My nails dig into his shoulders, my thighs clench around him, and the entire world shakes as I lose myself in the control he has on my body. A palm slaps across the curve of my ass, and my voice only becomes more muffled and ragged against Torben's chest.

"Good girl," Latham purrs, and then his hand grips my jaw, and he kisses me like he owns me. That same possessiveness pushes down my hips and rolls over my clit as he works me against his friend. A shiver races through me from his tone alone.

"Cum for him," Latham says along my lips.

The command alone is a dark sensation that rushes through my body on waves. That feeling lifts higher and higher. It builds deep within me. It all collides at once when Latham cups my sex with his palm and rocks against me from the front while his friend fucks me from the back.

My orgasm shatters so hard I tremble against all three of them. Aric's ragged groan stops long before he does. He doesn't stop until I'm cumming against him over and over again.

No one rushes me. Their hands caress across my skin in an intoxicating way, making me want more. I shove at Torben's jeans, and he's gentle with me as he lifts my hips and lines his thickness up beneath my swollen pussy. He takes his time. I feel him watching me while he ever so slowly slides in. Inch by inch, he fills me up. His cock is more than I need, but the sting of pain deep inside is a pleasure I can't explain.

My gasp is jagged, and his hum of cocky amusement is warm against my lips. Timid hands slide over my curves from behind, and I can't explain it, but I'd know that gentle touch anywhere.

Latham.

He's slow as he skims his palms back and forth across the curve of my ass as I rock against Torben's shaft. I sink down leisurely, loving every inch of his body against mine. Fingers tease me, sliding down the small of my back, my curves, and even lower. Latham's touch circles my ass, pressing deeper and deeper from behind. The pressure from the two of them is too much. I can't catch my breath.

But they're both so patient. Even as something cold presses against me. His finger slides in, curving just right. My moan

is taken in with the softest kiss. The hips beneath me grind up to meet my unsteadiness. Torben keeps me going while Latham works me at a torturously slow pace.

"Please," I beg in the heavy, breathy silence.

"Mmmm," is the only reply. Because then he's against me. Latham's slick cock slides in slowly. He pumps into me deeper and deeper on the slowest fucking pace that build so much deep within my core.

My cry of ecstasy is like nothing I've ever felt before. Conflicting pressure fills me up. Power blooms within like a storm ready to strike. Their hands hold me in place as Latham guides the rhythm of our bodies. His cock presses deep while Torben's grinds against me as well as him.

It feels slow and sweet and deep and dirty all at the same time. The two of them use me in the very best possible way until I'm trembling. I can't control my needy screams, my shaking breath, or the slamming of my release that pounds through me on an endlessness that never seems to stop.

I don't open my eyes to the starry spots that consume my vision until both of them slide from me moments later.

Rampant magic strikes through my veins, causing my shaking hands to feel even more out of control.

With no grace whatsoever, I slide off of Torben's lap and

fall against the man seated there against the wall.

Aric's smile is broad and beautiful when he wraps his arms around my shoulders. The three of them never take their eyes off of me.

I wish I could stay here in this bliss forever.

But my eyes are open now. And I'm sadly reminded that forever isn't really that long.

Minutes pass in silence as the swirling magic within me rolls on. Ready. Waiting.

"I still think I need to find her."

Torben clears his throat roughly.

"What?"

"Hela," Latham answers for me.

"She's the cause of this. We can help these people all we want, but we won't fix anything without finding her."

Aric shakes his head at me slowly. "She sent me and Kylie away to keep us busy in the Realm of Monsters. She sent all of us there to rot while she watches the world burn."

I blink at those words:

Watch the world burn.

"You're right." Even as I say it, his brows lift high as if no one's ever said those simple words to my crazy, demented dragon before.

"I am?"

I stumble to my feet and realize just how little balance I have after everything the four of us just did. My hands still shake with pent up power. I barely drag my jeans on before I'm piecing it all together.

"She's watching. She may not be here, but she'll see everything. Just like when I was lost in the maze with Torben, she won't miss out on watching the torment she's caused."

And I'm about to give her one hell of a show.

Chapter Eight

The Light

Rhys

I peer up at Bea. Golden sunlight casts over her like a martyr ready for remembrance. Her head hangs low, eyes softly shut, chest barely lifting with each inhale.

My fingers fist hard into my palm.

"She's safe," Latham tells me quietly, his hand sliding around my waist on a gentle touch.

Safe but suffering. All of these people are here untouched by a higher magic. Except for Bea, and I know—I just know—Hela's doing this to her because of me.

I'll save you, I vow internally.

Because I'll always remember how many times she saved me from myself as well as the pack who should have accepted me. And with that thought, I turn from her. As fast as my legs will carry me, I run out into the anarchy. Sparking magic deep in my chest seems to effect my speed. I'm even faster than I remember. Torben's on my heels before I've even made it ten yards though.

"Has she gone crazy?" Latham whispers under his breath just behind me.

"Definitely," Aric answers a bit too proudly.

I don't focus on them though. There's shoving and screaming all around. I don't hear any of it either. My eyes clench closed, and with every pounding step, I send out that powerful magic that I now fully understand. It's harnessed and ready. It drifts out of me like the sea lapping in to wash over the hot sand. A man holding an elderly gentleman by the collar draws his brows in confusion before slowly releasing him. I pass them by, and the crowd of angry women outside of a small flower shop lower their fists, their faces easing into that same dazed confusion as I race by.

This is it! It's working! I'm doing it!

"Shit. And all these years, Torben's been using his caveman

aggression, when all he needed was the power of love . . ."
Aric's laughter is cut off with a grunt, and I look back in
time to notice Torben's elbow jostling firmly into his
friend's ribs.

No! I don't have time for their distractions!

Without another thought, I throw myself forward. My arms
extend in midair, my legs lift with unknown power, and
then a full-fledged beast rips out of me. On four big white
paws, I land in my wolf's form like I've come home after
years of searching for it. There's no struggle to find her.
She and I are one, and as one, we storm out into the village.
Magic flows through my veins, and it's sent out faster than
I can process it.

The noise is muted. The world is blurred. Everything is
alive and numb all at the same damn time as my magic heals
what Hela had broken.

Hours slip by like that. It passes as quickly and as easily as
the wind blows.

I can see it though. Progress is being made.

Until…

A serpant rips from the ground. Grass and dirt fly up
through the air. Debris clouds my vision. Its head strikes at
me before I even see it coming. Sharp fangs nearly graze

my wolf's neck. Her body angles and we've barely leapt out of harms way in the nick of time.

I scatter out on four legs. My eyes narrow and I stand with confidence I've never felt in this form. She and I are the same. And we've crossed this motherfucker once before.

Serpan.

My lashing teeth snap at the beast. A shriek of a familiar bat cries above but a shaking roar is much closer. A shadow crosses over me from overhead. The scent of fire stings the air…

Then an enormous fiery dragon sweeps down from the heavens. His majestic wings pull in as he nose-dives down. And sharp black talons clamp over the snake's long, massive body.

With a proud roar the dragon soars off with his prey. It's all I can do to see them high in the sky before another attack is lashing out at me.

A large wolf, opposite of my pure white one circles me intently. I almost don't recognize the creature that once taunted me the night of the Dark Moon.

But my wolf would recognize her mate anywhere.

Kyvain's pale eyes are just as cruel as ever as he strides a slow, meaningful circle around me. With every lap, he

comes just a little closer. Just a little more and a little more and I know he's just searching out for his moment.

To leap.

And rip my fucking throat out once and for all.

His teeth bare and with a growl that reverberates through my entire body, it's me who strikes first. His neck is in my sights but he's too quick. He lunges and his shoulder is all I graze before he's put space between us. With quickness I search him out but hje's unseen. He's agile as he lashes out at me from behind. His big body takes me down. The weight of him alone is suffocating. I can't breathe. Darkness shadows over me, blinding me as I snap out at him sightlessly. Teeth sink in deep. The stab of pain shudders through my neck before hot blood pours down my throat. No matter how much I thrash, he outweighs me by too much.

Until that weight is tossed off of me. His teeth rip from my flesh and his whimper is all I hear before I stand, and see a fiery hellhound standing intently between me, and Kyvain. Latham's size is comparable to a family car. Kyvain looks from   me   to   the   hellhound. A limp jostles my steps as I walk forward and meet Latham at his side, both of us staring down the pathetic wolf cowering from the two of us now. Pain still stings at my throat but I ignore it.

He always did choose to harm anyone smaller than him. It's time for him to taste his own medicine.

"Ryhs," A deep voice calls out to me.

My ears twitch at that velvety voice alone and I look up at the warrior of man now at my side.

"The people need you," Torben stares intently into my eyes. "We got this. Keep going." And he's right.

Saving my pack is more important than my revenge on Kyvain. He'll get what he deserves.

That thought alone energizes as I rush out into the chaos once more. I expel it all to the people who probably don't even know my name. I give them every ounce of the magic I've saved up for just this very moment. Howls of wolves and roars of dragons flare up throughout my hours of running. With time it changes though. The fighting around me calms. They take my magic, my energy, my very soul it feels like.

Until there's nothing left.

Hues of pink and orange hit my lashes, and when my legs finally give out, I find myself in a full circle. My wolf retreats, and my knees hit the cold concrete of the battered pavilion.

Bea still hangs by her wrists. Her lips have a slight blue tint to them now, and even with all my energy and power waning, I still crawl to her. Trembling hands fumble. I only barely reach her feet with the tips of my fingers.

All that I have left, I expel against her freezing skin. The spine of my back stiffens, and I force my muscles to keep me held up just a bit longer. Magic rolls off of me and into her.

And then I drop.

My head hits the ground with a hard thud.

The dusty sky above is all I see for a while.

And then . . . her red-lipped smile comes into view where she stands over me.

"Good job," Hela coos, her slender hands clapping so slowly, they give off a slight echo. "Just cleared a population of four hundred. You could finish up the rest of California in a matter of months, I suppose. Just leaves . . . how many other states does this little nation own nowadays? What about Europe? Does she have any flyer miles to help her with the upcoming traveling she's going to have to commit to on this Love Tour of hers?" She peers back, and I have to strain to spot who she's speaking to.

Serpan's cackle slices through the sound of my labored breathing, but it's a much calmer, deeper voice who answers her. How is he even standing? Where's Aric?

Kyvain's body lies at Hela's feet. I can't tell if he's alive or dead but it's odd that he's here and Latham and Torben are not…

Fear burns through me at that thought.

I can't lift my head to look for them. I can only stare at this hellish woman consuming my vision.

"By the time the next village is cured, the last will have relapsed. Evil doesn't just *forget*. It doesn't rest. And it certainly doesn't stop." The elven king's smile is more charming and less genuine than Hela's.

But it's just as cruel.

I want to scream at them. I want to slam a knife through Hela's heart for all that she's done to the ones I love.

I just . . . can't lift my head to even look at her fully.

"You lost, Rhys. Just like the last Goddess of Love I came face to face with." The vindictive shine in her eyes is disgusting.

I fucking hate her!

"How about this?" Hela proposes with a casual clasp of her hands. "I'll take back your men. Consider it a reprimand for making me come down to this—" her lips curl as she looks around at the village, "*place*. I'll wash their memories of all this nastiness. I'll even halt the destruction of Ragnarök, and I'll let you all try it again. We can do this all again. And we'll see how long it takes for us to reconvene right here in your little village all over again. Shall we?"

"Fuck you," I hiss through dry lips.

"Rhys," someone says on a gentle tone.

And it cuts right through my heart. I'd know his warm voice anywhere. Even in the end of days.

Latham.

The back of my head scrapes over the concrete as I arch myself to look for him.

Only to find him as well as Aric and Torben bound in gleaming golden cuffs. They're anchored at the feet of the elven king. Hela's smile slices up in amusement when she notices my attention on them. Her long fingers stroke through Torben's beard as if he's her favorite pet.

No!" I scream, and my whole body shudders to lift up. My legs scramble beneath me but can't even crawl more than a few inches.

A delicate foot steps in front of me then. Silken, green slippers cover those feet. And a long shimmery dress skims the ground.

"You'll not talk to Goddess Love's daughter that way!" A slender elven woman lifts her head high, and it's then that I spot her friends surrounding me.

"Do not threaten me, Gnome!"

Goddess Love.

The memory of Loki's voice shifts through my mind: *The light elves do not offer kindness to outsiders. Not after what the Light King did to them . . .*

They loved my mother. And the elven king ruined their realm just like he ruined my mother.

Small hands press to my cold flesh. Dozens reach out to me, and it's as strange as it is whimsical. Their touch is magic to my senses. A buzz flicks over each and every nerve ending. A pure white glow casts from their fingertips and across my skin.

Something in them empowers me. It's a magic like no other, and it blinds my senses. That light intensifies until it burns up my surroundings. Nothing else exists. Only that light.

Soul Kissed

And her voice.

You are love. You are love. You are loved.

When I open my eyes once more, I'm standing among friends. Beasts of realms far and wide sit at my feet. Warrior women stand tall at my back. Light elves surround me on all sides. And there, to my left, is the God of Mischief.

Loki's smile isn't conniving and malicious as it normally is. It's sweet and kind.

"You remind me of her," he says reminiscently.

I peer down, and a white gown of thin, sparkling fabric covers my shimmering skin. Magic encompasses me. It shines right through me.

Because I'm a Goddess of Love.

Just as Loki once said.

I just never felt like it until now.

With a flash of my hand, I fling magic out, and a cracking of metal is the only sound as three sets of cuffs fall to the dirt. Aric's wide eyes peer over at Torben, but his gaze is focused entirely on me.

And he smiles.

My other hand lifts with intent, and with less force, I send out another wave of power. The gleaming chains around

Bea's hands crackle with anger when the chain splits open. Her feet falter, but Venus offers her support before she stumbles. Her bright but tired eyes beam at me as she's lowered to the ground.

"I want my realm returned to normal."

"That's—"

"I wasn't finished," I tell her flatly.

The Elfie king at her side narrows his eyes on me, but ultimately, no one speaks.

"You'll correct this realm. You'll leave this realm. And you'll never enter another of the Nine Realms ever again. You'll forever be a prisoner of your own misery."

Her laughter is a carrying clatter of amusement.

"You're just a girl."

"*A Goddess*," I correct.

"You don't have the authority to say who leaves and enters realms!"

"You're banned from the Light Realm," Loki chimes in.

"Muspelheim too," the leader of the Humnih says.

A warmth like love spreads all through my body, and I hold my head even higher.

"If I hear that another realm has been tormented by you or

your dog king, I'll come back to Hell for another visit."

The Elfie king rears his head back as if he's been slapped with a title no one has ever had the nerve to say to his arrogant face.

"You'd never make it past the DGE!" she snarls, her tone a bit more ruffled than usual.

The memory of the Department of Good and Evil flashes through my mind and the way I leapt with ease through that little office has me smiling.

"I'm not my mother, Hela. I'm not your king's prisoner. And if I broke into your realm once, I'll do it again." My gaze levels on her with a heaviness that I can't contain.

I want to break her. I want to rip her to shreds. I want her dead.

But taking away her ability to ruin other's lives, that's as good as dead.

And I see that when her smile finally falters. It slides off her face, and I love seeing her gaze shift from one person to the next within the crowd.

No one speaks up for her.

A ticking muscle spasms in her jaw just before she takes a solid step back. And with a flash of a hellish flame, she disappears.

A shrieking gasp sounds from Serpan, and those beady, little eyes of his look quickly to the elven king at his side. His mistress is gone. He's alone without her protection. The two of them pause, a slow second slipping by before their attention lifts. Several light elves take slow steps forward.

Loki tsks at them. "Now, now, friends." His chuckle is cruel and sinister. "Get him!" he beckons.

And with never before seen haste, the king rushes off into the rubble of the village, Serpan's wailing following quickly after.

A popping noise signals so loudly, I instantly follow the sound. Kyvain's lifeless body sizzles out into black, inky smoke.

He's gone.

What else is gone? Is that Hela's magic healing this world?

The chains at Bea's feet pop loudly. They too disappear. The three sets of cuffs do the same. A cold wind blows hard. The debris of rocks at my feet clatter around me, coming together ever so slowly, to fix what was once broken.

The sounds of Serpan's screams and the king's storming

boots fade out. Everything is silent for a second.

Everything feels almost normal.

Or as normal as it can be.

I hope . . . I want to hope he dies by the hands of those feral little elves.

But I'm happy not to know.

Sometimes not knowing is bliss.

And sometimes . . . I peer up to the only men who have ever loved me. Their gazes pull to me magnetically with warmth searing across my glowing flesh from their attention alone.

Sometimes bliss is more than you've ever known.

Epilogue

Three Months Later

Rhys

"Thing's a demon!"

"Straight from Hell," Latham agrees.

Aric and Latham both stand in front of the large second-story window of our little apartment, but it isn't until I push past them that I see what they're glaring at.

"Aww, you got Loki a cat tree!" I pick up the little black cat and place it higher on the carpeted stand.

"Was on sale," Torben grunts from the couch.

He sits at the center, and though it's a full-sized piece of furniture, it might as well be a child's toy that he's sitting on. We got it the night we moved in. The three men of Hell got me a little apartment miles away from the Dark Moon Pack. I'm close enough to see Bea on the weekends, and far enough away to never have to be under an Alpha's authority ever again.

They said I didn't belong there.

They're right.

I belong with them. After everything I've been through, and after all that I've lost, their love eases the pain. I'll never fully know my mother. I've never had a family.

But we have us.

I carry the purring pet across the room, and a big hand pulls me down. Torben jostles me onto his lap before I can even pick a seat.

Aric takes the one on my left. Latham on the right.

Popcorn is tossed over my head, and another food fight is about to ensue between the two biggest man children that have ever escaped Hell. A smile warms my lips as Torben clicks on the television. Laughter hums through the room, and I rest my head back against a Warrior God's strong chest.

And we binge watch TV for the rest of the night.

Because life is fucking peaceful.

Finally.

"I'm kind of sad your glowy skin wore off," Latham whispers when a chorus of credits cuts across the screen.

"It was nothing special," I say.

"It was a little neat," Torben says against my neck.

"No. It was nothing special." I shrug as he hugs me harder.

Aric's laughter is heard long before his reply. "Yeah right. Looked like a rave every time we fuc—"

The Hellish End.

Soul Kissed

Also by A.K. Koonce

Reverse Harem Books

The To Tame a Shifter Series

Taming

Claiming

Maiming

Sustaining

Reigning

The Monsters and Miseries Series

Hellish Fae

Sinless Demons

A. K. Koonce

Spiteful Creatures

The Villainous Wonderland Series

Into the Madness

Within the Wonder

Under the Lies

Origins of the Six

Academy of Six

Control of Five

Destruction of Two

Wrath of One

The Hopeless Series

Hopeless Magic

Soul Kissed

Hopeless Kingdom

Hopeless Realm

Hopeless Sacrifice

The Secrets of Shifters

The Darkest Wolves

The Sweetest Lies

The Royal Harem Series

The Hundred Year Curse

The Curse of the Sea

The Legend of the Cursed Princess

The Severed Souls Series

Darkness Rising

A. K. Koonce

Darkness Consuming

Darkness Colliding

The Huntress Series

An Assassin's Death

An Assassin's Deception

An Assassin's Destiny

Dr. Hyde's Prison for the Rare

Escaping Hallow Hill Academy

Surviving Hallow Hill Academy

Paranormal Romance Books

The Cursed Kingdoms Series

Soul Kissed

The Cruel Fae King

The Cursed Fae King

The Crowned Fae Queen

The Twisted Crown Series

The Shadow Fae

The Iron Fae

The Lost Fae

The Midnight Monsters Series

Fate of the Hybrid, Prequel

To Save a Vampire, Book one

To Love a Vampire, Book two

To Kill a Vampire, Book three

About A. K. Koonce

A.K. Koonce is a USA Today bestselling author. She's a mom by day and a fantasy and paranormal romance writer by night. She keeps her fantastical stories in her mind on an endless loop while she tries her best to focus on her actual life and not that of the spectacular, but demanding, fictional characters who always fill her thoughts.

Soul Kissed

Printed in Great Britain
by Amazon